Say Hello, Lily

To my family, and to my friends at
the Sarah Chudnow Campus
—D.L.

For my dear Caro
—M.A.

KAR-BEN Publishing, Inc.
A division of Lerner Publishing Group
241 First Avenue North
Minneapolis, MN 55401 U.S.A.
800-4KARBEN

Website address: www.karben.com

Library of Congress Cataloging-in-Publication Data

Lakritz, Deborah.
     Say hello, Lily / by Deborah Lakritz ; illustrated by Martha Aviles.
        p.   cm.
     Summary: Lily wants to go with her mother to visit the people who live at Shalom
House, an assisted living facility, but when they arrive she suddenly feels very shy.
     ISBN: 978-0-7613-4511-4 (lib. bdg. : alk. paper) [1. Old age—Fiction.
2. Bashfulness—Fiction.] I. Avilés Junco, Martha, ill. II. Title.
PZ7.L15934Say 2010
[E]—dc22   2009001873

Manufactured in the United States of America
1 – BP – 7/15/10

Say Hello, Lily

By
Deborah Lakritz

Illustrated by
Martha Avilés

KAR-BEN
PUBLISHING

"Take me!" said Lily one afternoon, as Mommy reached for her car keys.

"But today's my day to volunteer at Shalom House. Lots of people you don't know will want to talk to you," her mom said, knowing how shy Lily was. "Are you sure you want to come?"

Lily grabbed her jacket. "I want to come! I'll draw pictures for everyone with my new markers. And I can show off my new shoes."

In the back seat of the car, Lily clutched her box of markers and pad of paper. She clicked her shoes together.

"Mommy, what *is* Shalom House?" she asked.

Mommy smiled. "It's a place for older people to live if they need extra help. Remember our neighbor Mrs. Rosenbaum, the artist? She had trouble climbing all those stairs in her house, and after she stopped driving she was very lonely."

Lily nodded.

"Now she lives in an apartment at Shalom House. There are no more stairs to climb. When she wants to go someplace, she can ride in the Shalom House van. And if she wants company, there are always people nearby."

Lily remembered that Mrs. Rosenbaum had an art studio in her house. "My favorite painting was a vase of orange flowers," said Lily, who dreamed of being an artist someday. "Remember, Mommy? She said they were lilies—like me! I hope we see her today, and I hope she still has her paintings."

Mommy parked the car. As they walked into Shalom House, Lily's new shoes *clip-clopped* along the entrance ramp.

In the lobby, smiling faces popped up everywhere, faces Lily had never seen before. Suddenly she felt jumbled up inside. Her heart thumped and her face turned red. She reached for her mother's hand.

"Look at your beautiful new shoes," said Mrs. Seidel,
leaning on her walker. "I used to sell shoes just like
yours when I owned my own store."

"How about a smile?" said Dr. Berman, kneeling down. "When I was a dentist I loved to see my patients show off their clean, shiny teeth."

"Say hello, Lily," said Mommy. Lily looked down at the floor.

"Be patient," said a lady holding a drawing pad. *"She'll be ready when she's ready."*

"Mrs. Rosenbaum!" said Mommy. "Lily remembers visiting your house and seeing your beautiful paintings."

"I still have them," said Mrs. Rosenbaum. "Maybe one day you'll stop by my apartment and see them."

Lily peeked out from behind Mommy. "Do you think she still has the painting of the lilies?" Lily whispered.

"You'll have to see for yourself," said Mommy.

The next week when Lily visited Shalom House, there was an exercise class going on in the social hall.

"Stretch, two, three, four! Come join us," the instructor called. Lily stepped backwards.

"Don't slip in those fancy shoes," said Mrs. Seidel, her arms stretched overhead.

"I'll bet I can make you smile," said Dr. Berman, kicking his leg up in the air.

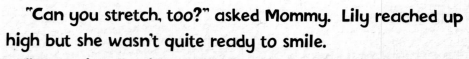

"Can you stretch, too?" asked Mommy. Lily reached up high but she wasn't quite ready to smile.

"Be patient," said Mrs. Rosenbaum, trying to touch her toes. "She'll be ready when she's ready."

The next week when Lily arrived, the lobby buzzed with people. Music played over the loudspeakers. Balloons floated overhead.

"Just in time!" said Sally, the social director. "We're throwing a party for residents with May birthdays.

Lily's stomach flip-flopped. Her heart skipped a beat. *Her* birthday was in May!

"You're wearing your party shoes," said Mrs. Seidel.

"Today I can see your smile!" said Dr. Berman, tapping his foot to the music.

"That's because *my* birthday is in May, too!" said Lily, taking a step closer to the party table.

"You can be my helper," Sally said. Lily
beamed as she passed out plates of chocolate
cake and cups of punch. When she reached
Mrs. Rosenbaum, Lily began to talk.

"*My* birthday's next week," she told her.
"*I'm* having a party, too!"
"Party? Can I come? I love parties!"
teased Mrs. Rosenbaum. Lily giggled.

That night, Lily took out her markers and paper. She drew and colored, and colored and drew. Then she carefully folded each picture and put it in an envelope.

Before bed, Lily handed her mom a pile of colorful envelopes. "I know what I want for my birthday," she said, showing her what she had drawn.

"I'll see what I can do," Mommy said.

On the morning of her birthday, Lily galloped
down the stairs.

"Let's go!" she said, grabbing her jacket.

Daddy carried her cake out to the car.
Mommy stuffed a bundle of balloons into the
trunk. Lily climbed into the back seat, clicking
her party shoes.

When they arrived at Shalom House, smiling faces popped up everywhere.

This time, Lily felt butterflies fluttering inside. Her heart flipped with joy.

"Happy birthday, Lily," said Mrs. Seidel. "I see you're wearing your birthday shoes."

"Happy birthday, Lily," said Dr. Berman. "I see you're wearing your birthday smile."

"You got the invitations I made!" Lily exclaimed.

Her mom lit the candles, and her new friends sang "Happy Birthday." Lily passed out birthday cake and punch.

After the party, Mrs. Rosenbaum put her arm around Lily.
"Come to my apartment. I have a surprise."

When they walked through the door, Lily couldn't believe
her eyes. The beautiful paintings she remembered from Mrs.
Rosenbaum's house covered all the walls of the apartment.
But something was missing.

"Where is the painting of the
orange flowers?" Lily asked Mrs.
Rosenbaum.
   "You'll have to see for yourself,"
she replied, handing Lily a big
package. "Happy birthday!"

The paper crinkled as Lily opened her present.
"The orange flowers!" she said excitedly. "For me?"
"Can you show me how to draw flowers like these?" asked Lily.

"Are you sure you're ready?" asked
Mrs. Rosenbaum, her eyes twinkling.
    Lily watched as she opened a drawer
and took out some markers and a pad
of paper.
    "Yes, Mrs. Rosenbaum. *Now* I'm ready!"

About the Author
and Illustrator

Deborah Lakritz

has a Masters Degree in Social Work from
the University of Minnesota. She has worked
professionaly with both pre-schoolers
and senior citizens. She lives in Milwaukee,
Wisconsin with her husband, five children,
and pet fish, Sunny.

Martha Avilés

was born and raised in Mexico City and has
been an illustrator since her daughter was a
little girl. Martha loves the moon and the rain
and admires and honors the souls of the old.